S0-ARC-020

DISCARD

PETUNIA

PETUNIA

Written and illustrated by
ROGER DUVOISIN

DRAGONFLY BOOKS · ALFRED A. KNOPF
NEW YORK

Jenkins Creek Elem. Library
26915 - 186th Ave. S.E.
Kent, WA 98042

A DRAGONFLY BOOK PUBLISHED BY ALFRED A. KNOPF, INC.
Copyright © 1950 by Alfred A. Knopf, Inc.
Copyright renewed 1977 by Roger Duvoisin
All rights reserved under International and Pan-American Copyright Conventions. Published in
the United States by Alfred A. Knopf, Inc., New York, and simultaneously in Canada by Random House
of Canada Limited, Toronto. Distributed by Random House, Inc., New York. Originally published in
hardcover by Alfred A. Knopf, Inc., in 1950.
Library of Congress Catalog Card Number: 72-9552
ISBN: 0-394-82589-6
Manufactured in the United States of America
2 3 4 5 6 7 8 9

In the meadow, early one morning, Petunia, the silly goose,
went strolling. She ate a bug here, clipped off a clover leaf
there, and she picked at the dewdrops on the goldenrod leaves.

Then, suddenly, she saw something she had never seen before in the meadow. What was it?

Petunia stole closer and closer
and sniffed at it from all sides.

"By Goosey Gander," she said, "it does not
smell like food for a goose. But I believe I
have seen such a thing before. . . .

"Yes, I have seen one under Bill's arm when he came out of school. It's a Book. That's it. A BOOK!

"Come to think of it, just the other day I heard Mr. Pumpkin telling Bill that Books are very precious. 'He who owns Books and loves them is wise.' That is what he said.

6

"He who owns Books and loves them is wise," repeated Petunia to herself. And she thought as hard and as long as she could. "Well, then," she said at last, "if I take this Book with me, and love it, I will be wise too. And no one will call me a silly goose ever again."

So Petunia picked up the Book, and off she went with it.

She slept with it . . .   she swam with it.

And, knowing that she was so wise, Petunia also became proud,

and prouder   and prouder. . .   so proud

that her neck stretched out several notches.

It was King, the rooster, who first noticed the change in
Petunia. He said, "Maybe Petunia is not so silly after all. She has
a Book. And she looks so wise that she must be so."

And the other animals began to believe in Petunia's wisdom
too. They asked her for advice and opinions, and Petunia was
glad to help—even when she was not asked.

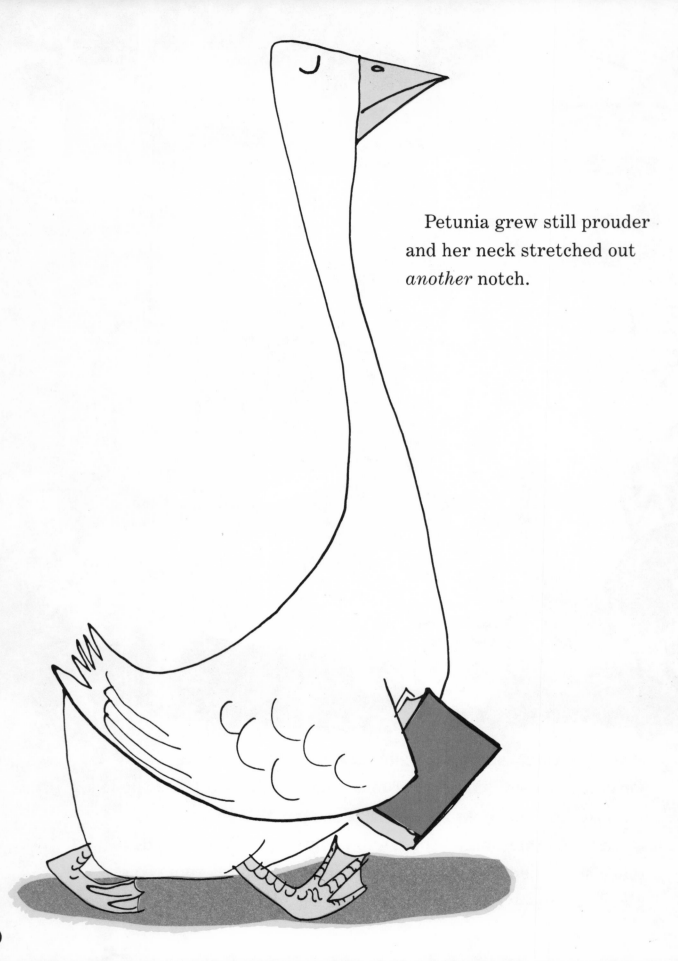

Petunia grew still prouder
and her neck stretched out
another notch.

One day Petunia heard Clover, the cow, say to King, the
rooster, "I wonder what makes your comb so red, King—as red
as the barn."

"It's my blood," said King. "It's the color of my blood."

"Nonsense," said Clover. "I have blood too. But I'm not a red
cow. Your comb has been dipped in red barn-paint, that's what
makes it so red."

"You are both silly, of course," said Petunia. "King, your comb
was stuck on by the farmer so he can tell you from the hens and
know who lays eggs and who doesn't. Plastic comb, I'd say."

And so King never again shook his proud comb in song for fear
it might fall off.

Poor sad rooster.

But Petunia had other things to do.

At the chicken coop, Ida, the hen, was cackling excitedly among her chicks. "Oh, Petunia," she said, "my chicks and I have been for a walk in the woods, and I think I've lost some of them. The farmer says I had nine but I can't count so very well. Please, wise Petunia, count my chicks to see if they're all here."

"Glad to help," said Petunia. "Hm. Let's see. Three chicks at the fountain. Three at the feeder. Three about your legs. Now— three times three? That makes six . . ."

"Six?" asked Ida. "Six! Is that less than nine?"

"That's *more* than nine, not less," said Petunia. "*Lots* more, my dear!"

"*More than nine?* Good gracious! As if I hadn't enough worries with my own nine chicks. And where do those other chicks come from? Oh, dear, I'll never be happy again."

Poor worried Ida.

But Petunia had other things to do.

In the meadow she discovered part of Noisy, the dog, sticking out of a hole in the ground.

"Help! Help!" cried Noisy. "I stuck my head in this rabbit hole, and now it won't come out. Help!"

"Glad to help," said Petunia. "It's a good thing I know what hunters do to get stubborn animals out of holes in the ground. They *smoke* them out. Wait until I fetch some sticks and some matches."

And so, wise Petunia built a fire in the other end of the hole and fanned it well with the Book.

Her trick worked nicely. Noisy, choking with smoke, jerked his head out of the hole and ran off howling with pain. His nose was singed with the fire, and his ears were cut and bruised.

Poor moaning dog.

JENKINS CREEK ELEM. LIBRARY

But Petunia had other things to do.

Beside the hedgerow she met Straw, the horse, who was in pain from a toothache.

"Petunia," groaned Straw, "I'm dying. Surely, with your wisdom, you can stop this horrible pain."

"Glad to help," said Petunia. "Open your mouth. Why . . . you poor Straw . . . all these teeth! No wonder you have a toothache.

"Look at me. Do I have teeth? Of course not. So I have no toothache. I am going to stop that pain right now. I am going to pull *all* those teeth out. *All* of them. Let me get some pliers . . ."

But Straw would not wait for the pliers. He was so afraid to lose his teeth that he never talked of his toothache to another soul. He suffered in silence.

Poor forlorn horse.

But Petunia had other things to do.

Cotton, the kitten, went up the tree but could not come down. While he miaowed and miaowed, his friends called for Petunia.

"Glad to help," said Petunia. "I know just what to do. Since none of you is tall enough to reach Cotton, all of you will do it together. Donkey on top of Clover, Pig on top of Donkey, and so on up. Simple."

So Donkey climbed on top of Clover;
Pig on top of Donkey;
Goat on top of Pig;
Sheep on top of Goat;
Piggy on top of Sheep;
Turkey on top of Piggy;
Duck on top of Turkey;
Hen on top of Duck. . . .
Suddenly Clover cried out,
"Stop! My legs feel wobbly."
And she sat . . .

. . . and Donkey and the rest
fell into a heap, and
Cotton was so scared that
he fell on top of them.
They were all full of bumps.

"Well," said Petunia, "Cotton
is *down*."

So he was, poor bruised kitten.

But Petunia had other things to do. Getting prouder all the
time, she felt her neck stretch further out.

She now wandered down the meadow, where she found some other friends gathered around a box.

"Ah, wise Petunia!" they shouted. "We found this box in the ditch beside the road. Maybe it's food, Petunia. Please tell us what the writing on it says."

"Glad to help," said Petunia. "Now, let's see . . . Why, CANDIES. That's what it says on that box. Yes, candies. You may eat them. Yes, of course."

No sooner had Petunia given the word than seven greedy
mouths tore up the box and grabbed the candies out of it,
and . . .

BOOM

What a sight the animals were!

Some were burned.

Some were bruised.

Straw still suffered in silence.

Noisy still moaned.

Ida still worried about her chicks.

King still brooded over his comb.

All the barnyard was in trouble, and all because of Petunia.

Petunia's pride and wisdom had exploded with the firecrackers.

Her neck had shrunk back to its old size and was all bandaged up. She was the most downhearted of all, for she saw now that she was not a bit wise.

But suddenly Petunia spied the Book. The firecrackers had blown it open so that the pages showed. She had never seen them before. Now she saw that there was something written inside the Book which she could not read. So she sat down and thought and thought and thought, until at last she sighed, "Now I understand. It was not enough to carry wisdom under my wing. I must put it in my mind and in my heart. And to do that I must learn to read."

Petunia was filled with joy. At once she began to work so that one day she could be truly wise. Then she would help make her friends happy.